ADORABLE FAT GIRL AT CHRISTMAS

BERNICE BLOOM

Bernice Bloom

ADORABLE FAT GIRL

AT CHRISTMAS

By Bernice Bloom

LETTER TO MY LOVELY READERS

HAPPY CHRISTMAS (if it is Christmas, if it isn't - thank you for being a maverick and unconstrained by the seasons. I hope you're reading this on a lovely beach somewhere),

Thank you so much for buying my latest mini book, in which our rather bonkers heroine embraces Christmas with all the delight and joy of a toddler spotting a large chocolate cake. She causes chaos wherever she goes (of course), with a naivety and joy that allows others to forgive her indiscretions.

This little bundle of pages features the Beckhams' Christmas tree, lots of booze, two Christmas lunches and a wild & entirely inaccurate confession to Holly Willoughby.

The series now contains dozens of books, including comedy books, mystery books and weightless books, so if you enjoy this one, there are loads more to try.

Also, look out for more books in the future, launching every couple of months. All the details are on:

www.bernicebloom.com.

They are available to buy here: https://www.amazon.co.

uk/Bernice-Bloom/e/B01MPZ5SBA/ref=
sr_ntt_srch_lnk_2?qid=1478133414&sr=1-2

I hope you all have a brilliant, fun & laughter-filled Christmas (or summer, or Easter, or Wednesday...or whatever day of the week, month and year it is!).

Thanks so much for your support.

Lots of love,

Bernie x

PS Email me on bernicenovelist@gmail.com if you have any queries about the books

CHAPTER ONE

FOSTERS DIY STORE

"*M*ary Brown, Mary Brown. Please go to the store manager's office. The store manager's office, immediately."

Oh bloody hell, this isn't going to be good. I put down the spades that I am arranging in height order in the gardening section (I'm just trying to look busy - there's no reason on God's earth why the spades should be assembled in height order), and I waddle out of the huge conservatory past the rows of plants and into the main part of the store, heading to the manager's office.

I'm wearing my bright green overalls and a red hat and gloves. I don't think anyone has ever looked less attractive (I resemble a large, wobbly poinsettia which is kind of festive - but that's the only good thing you could say about it). It's just so cold over in the gardening section that looking good is right at the bottom of the 'things I care about' list. It's hard to think about style when you're struggling not to shiver.

I'm only in the gardening section this week because I said that I wanted to be around all the Christmas trees and the holly and mistletoe. I thought it would be all Christmassy

1

and fun in there, but they haven't even got one tree that's nicely decorated at the store, or any Christmas music or lights or any of the lovely Christmassy things you need to make the place look great.

This distresses me a considerable amount because I love Christmas, I mean I REALLY LOVE Christmas. If I were running this place all the staff would be dressed like Santa and giving out presents to kids, singing carols and being jolly and friendly. The other staff I've spoken to don't agree. They say that most people just want to come into a DIY shop, buy a hammer and go home - not be confronted by a bunch of idiots singing 'We wish you a Merry Christmas' in home-made tinsel hats, and handing out ugly stuffed toys. I think people do though. I think people love Christmas and want things to be special...even if it's just going into the DIY shop to buy nails. You want everything you do to have a sprinkle of Chjristmas on it.

"Oohh, someone's in trouble," says Neil as I pass him by the shelving aisle.

He's obviously heard the announcement calling me to the manager's office and assumes that I've done something wrong.

"No, Keith wants to talk to me about a pay rise," I say.

"Yeah right," says Neil. "Because Keith is *always* doing that."

I give him a smile and a shrug of my shoulders, but Neil's probably right. I am bound to be in trouble. Why else would I be summoned over the public address system? It'll be because of my joke yesterday. A guy was buying a screwdriver in the hardware section and I was working on the tills. He came over to pay and as I put the digits into the card machine, his phone rang. It really made me laugh because it was as if I'd just dialled him, so I picked up the card reader and pretended it was a phone...holding it to my ear and saying, 'Hello, anyone there.' In my head it was very funny, and to the guy's credit he did laugh weakly at me when I did it. The trouble was, when I brushed the machine against my ear, I managed to add extra zeros to the total, and the screwdriver ended up costing £1900. It was quite a fiasco when his bank rejected the payment, then we realised what I'd done. He wasn't laughing so much then.

I'm pretty sure that'll be what Keith wants to discuss with me - my wholly unprofessional behaviour.

Or it could have been the lipstick kisses I put on the paint mixing forms. Oh God - yes, I'd forgotten about those. Once people have paid for their paint, we give them a form with the details of the paint they have ordered on it...a kind of receipt. Well, I put lipstick kisses on the bottom of them and was told in no uncertain terms that my actions were inappropriate.

I walk into Keith's office and decide to front up straight away in the hope that this will minimise the anger he feels towards me.

"Listen, I'm sorry about the lipstick kisses," I say. "I know that was unprofessional, but the customers didn't object at all. No one complained. It was a bit of light-hearted fun."

"What lipstick kisses?" he asks.

Oh no.

"Um. Well, I was working on the paint mixing counter and when people place an order, we give them a receipt and tell them to come back in an hour to collect the paint."

"Yes, I know you do, Mary. I implemented that system."

"Well, I put 'see you in an hour' and a lipstick kiss - it was just a bit of fun...I thought that's what you wanted to see me about."

"Er...no," says Keith, with a bemused look on his red face."I'm calling you in because I want you to be in charge of Christmas."

"In charge of Christmas? What do you mean?"

This sounds like the best job in the world, ever.

"You know - make the store look Christmassy, organise some Christmas events, make a list of all the things you think we should be doing to make this the best store in the world this Christmas. Do you think you're up to it?"

"Oh God, yes," I say, rising to my feet and just about resisting the urge to throw my arms around his thick, florid neck and kiss his bald patch. "I've never been up for anything more in my entire life."

"Good," he says. "Have a ponder and come back to me with a list of what you think we ought to be doing."

"I will," I say, beaming.

"Oh, and Mary,"

"Yes."

"Stop doing that lipstick kiss thing."

"Ofcourse," I say. "Sorry. I won't do it again."

I walk out of Keith's office and do a little jig. Not a big, full-on dance or anything - I'm British, after all - just a small shuffle to reflect the happiness that is bubbly up inside me. Then I smile deeply to myself and think - I'm only in charge of bloody Christmas.

CHAPTER TWO

BATTLE OF THE PARENTS

I get home from work, still wholly preoccupied by my great new role in life, and the phone is ringing in my flat. I always answer the landline with extreme caution because it's usually someone trying to sell me something or convince me that I've been in an accident that wasn't my fault. There have been times when the woman on the phone is so convincing that I come away believing that I have been in an accident. Maybe someone has knocked into my car and I wasn't at fault? It could have happened. Then I remember that I can't drive and don't have a car.

"Hello Mary, it's mum."

Yes - that's the other thing I should have mentioned about the landline: if it's not a salesman, it's mum. Really - everyone else in the entire world now rings me on my mobile, but not my mother.

"I'm in charge of Christmas!" I blurt out. There's a moment's silence.

"Very good," she says, before moving on. "As a special treat, we thought it would be nice to invite Ted to come to us for Christmas. Do you think he'd like to?"

I have to tell you - this is a most unusual development. My Dad is normally so unsociable, you wouldn't believe it. For mum to invite anyone round, knowing what dad's like, is a miracle...for them to invite a boyfriend of mine...someone they haven't even met yet...well, that's plain unheard of.

"I think he'd love to," I say, feeling a shiver of excitement at the thought of waking up on Christmas morning in my flat with Ted then walking hand-in-hand with him to mum and dad's house.

"Good," says mum. "Then I'll make sure we have enough food in for all of us. I told your father that I was inviting Ted and he said he was looking forward to meeting him."

I know this isn't true. Dad hates meeting anyone new.

"Oh, and we're getting a new freezer. Did I tell you?"

Again, this is surprising news. For most people, a new freezer might not be a huge deal, but for mum and dad - it's bigger news than if she told me that dad was getting a sex change. They don't ever buy anything new. They are all about 'make do and mend' - it's like the Blitz is going on, and they feel duty bound not to use up the country's precious, dwindling resources.

"We've been talking about it for a few years now, and we're going to get one before Christmas. Will you help me choose one?"

"Of course I will," I say.

"Very good. Talk to you soon."

Whenever I speak to mum on the phone I'm astonished by how clipped her tones are, and how formal and profession she sounds; it's as if she's talking on a telephone for the first time ever. As if phones have just been invented and she's really not at all sure whether they're a good idea. She's not at all like that in real life. Still - really nice of her to invite Ted to Christmas. I'm chuffed about that.

. . .

LATER THAT EVENING I arrive at Ted's flat, eager to give him the double helping of good news that I have been put in charge of Christmas, and that he has been invited to spend Christmas Day with me and my parents. I'm not sure how he'll react to the latter of these two pieces of information because he's never met my parents...I've kind of kept them separate on purpose because my dad can be hard work. But now that Ted and I have been going out together for six months, it's definitely time he met them, and Christmas will be the perfect opportunity.

He opens the door and he's beaming with delight. It's like he knows my good news.

"You look happy," I say.

"I'm very happy, young lady," he says, pulling me into his arms. "Come in and I'll tell you all about it."

Ted closes the door behind me and I start walking up the narrow staircase to his flat. I hate walking ahead of Ted. I'm always worried that he's looking at my huge bottom and wondering whether he'd really be better off with someone whose bottom wasn't the size of a large freight ship. I worry that he'll go off me or something. Not that he's thin. We met at Fat Club and are both clinically obese. We've lost some weight and are on mad diets most of the time, but we still both weigh twice what a normal person does.

We get to the top (which is only about 10 steps) and I'm breathing heavily...I really need to start exercising as well as dieting.

"I'm in charge of Christmas!" I blurt out.

"OK, you'll never guess where we've been invited," he says.

Why is no one in the world reacting in the way I expect them to act to the news that I am IN CHARGE OF CHRIST-MAS. Surely that statement deserves some recognition, but first mum completely ignored me, now Ted is completely ignoring me.

"I'm in charge of Christmas," I repeat.

"I know," he says. "You said. Well done, you. Now - you have to guess where we've been invited to go."

Clearly no one is anywhere near as excited by my news as I am.

"Buckingham Palace?" I venture.

"Better."

"Better than Buckingham Palace? Um...The White House? Is that better? I don't know. Tell me."

"OK. Wait for this...you know how bloody unsociable my mum and dad are? Well...they have invited us to have Christmas lunch with them. I can't believe it. It's so exciting. My sister's away for Christmas and they thought we might like to join them instead. Please, please, please say 'yes'."

"Um... yes," I say, before I can stop myself, and explain that I have already committed us to lunch at my parents, and they, too, are terribly unsociable, and an invitation to anyone to join in is as rare as hen's teeth. But I don't want to let Ted down; he looks so excited. And it is great that his parents have invited me to join them for Christmas. I'm flattered. Perhaps I can pull out later...urge him to change his mind and come with me to mum and dad's instead.

"Brilliant," he says, gathering me up and kissing me all over my face. "You've made me the happiest man alive. Now I can't wait for Christmas day. It's going to be the best ever."

Shit.

We retire to bed with glasses of wine, with Ted abuzz and beaming with happiness that we will be spending Christmas at his mum's, and me desperately trying to look like it's a great idea, and not to look as if I just committed us to Christmas at my mum's.

"What did you say earlier?" he asks. "Something about you wanting to take charge of Christmas."

"No, I've taken charge of Christmas. I am now in charge. It's official."

"I think you'll find Father Christmas already has that job sewn up, sweetheart. What are you talking about?"

"I'm talking about work...Keith called me into his office today and has told me that he wants me to be in charge of Christmas."

"Wow, that's brilliant," says Ted.

Finally, someone recognises what a big deal this is!

"You'll be perfect."

"Yes - I know. I'm beyond excited about it," I say. "I have so many plans for decorating the store, and offering a Christmas tree decorating service and lollipops for children..."

"It all sounds great," says Ted, kissing me lightly on the cheek and preparing to roll over and go to sleep. "Goodnight Mary Christmas," he says, and I drift off to sleep, thinking of how to make Fosters DIY Emporium the best Christmas experience ever.

We need a nativity scene...a brilliant one. Perhaps we should have real donkeys. Where can you get real donkeys from? Obviously we need a huge Christmas tree with beautiful lights, presents underneath it and a star on top, and we need lots of Father Christmases and carols playing and sweets for children and the smell of mulled wine and mince pies, and maybe Christmas cards for every customer. And baby Jesus. I'll need a baby. Can you hire them? I need to check that. I'll do it all in the morning. I'll make this the best Christmas ever for everyone who comes into the store.

CHAPTER THREE

BEING MARY CHRISTMAS

*B*y 9am the next morning, after a fitful night's sleep which was interrupted by the arrival of Christmas thoughts, plans and themes flooding into my mind, I find myself standing in front of Keith with my list of ideas.

"Here's my list of Christmas events that we could host in the store," I say. "And some business ideas and decoration ideas." Keith is nodding happily and saying all the right things. What he's worried about, of course, is the cost.

"I thought maybe we could get the local paper to come down," I say. "If the store looks good enough, they'll come. They like Christmas pictures in the paper, don't they? If we had an amazing Christmas scene, they might come down and photograph it, then we'd be in the papers and we'd attract more customers. Then your boss would be really happy."

You see: I may look stupid in my large green overall and with Christmas decorations hanging from my ears (are they too much?), but I'm not. I know that the prospect of free publicity will be enough to compel him to spend a fortune.

"Indeed," says Keith, with a sharp rise of his eyebrows.

"Very good thinking. And then we can offset the costs against the PR budget. Perfect. Get to it, Mary. I want you to price all of this lot up and let me know how much you think it will cost. Christmas is in six days so we need to get cracking."

"Great," I say, standing up and adjusting the tinsel in my hair (now that really might be too much, but I couldn't resist). "The only thing is - I'm supposed to be working on the till in the bathroom section this afternoon. It will take a while to do all this. Could someone else cover, so I can sit down and sort this out."

"Yes, of course," says Keith, hitting the microphone and buzzer on his desk. "Could the supervisor working in the bathrooms section please come to the manager's office immediately. Thank you," he says.

"Mary, go and work on the desk next to Sharon and let me know how much it will all cost and how long it will take. Let's try and get this place Christmas-ed up to the hilt by the end of the day, and I want photographers and BBC news film crews here tomorrow."

"Right," I say. He seems to have escalated the publicity potential in his mind. My suggestion of a local newspaper has been replaced by the 10 O'clock news. How do you convince a TV crew to come to a DIY store? Presumably they have better things to do. Presumably they wouldn't come unless a child was kidnapped or something?

I take a seat next to perfect Sharon in her elegant cream suit (not for her the daily humiliation of a green overall because she's the manager's PA), and I start scribbling.

The first thing I have to do is create a very realistic nativity scene. I'll need a baby, a Mary and Jesus, wise men, shepherds and some animals. That can't be too hard to assemble, can it? I mean - the average junior school production manages to acquire all of those, so it can't be beyond me.

"It's nice to have a girl working alongside me," says

Sharon, in her nauseatingly feminine voice (only nauseating because all the men seem to adore her high-pitched, adolescent squeaks. I'm not a fan - she sounds like she's been inhaling laughing gas).

"Yes," I say with my head bowed over my notebook, trying to write without the Christmas bauble earrings I'm wearing bashing into the Santa Claus pen I'm clutching (yes, I'm aware that I'm taking this whole 'in charge of Christmas' thing incredibly seriously).

Sharon is looking at me.

"Mary, you might be able to help me with this," she says. "Something's been really troubling me."

"Has it?"

"Yes, I saw on the tele last night that they said one in three men lives at home now."

"OK," I say. "That doesn't surprise me. It's a sign of the times...credit crunch and all that. People are finding it difficult to buy their own homes."

"No, but it's ridiculous...everyone lives at home."

"Yes, but what they mean is that one in three men lives in the family home rather than buying their own home."

"But it's still a home."

"You're right," I say. "How silly of them."

"Isn't she adorable?" says Keith, standing over Sharon as we chat. "Mary, we're very lucky to have someone as smart and lovely as Sharon in the office."

"We are," I say, looking up at him as he grins down at her and she turns scarlet in response. Keith does have more than a touch of the David Brents to him. Everything he does is ever-so lightly cringey.

"Come on Sharon, let me take you out to lunch as a Christmas treat. Mary, maybe you could man the office while we're out?"

"Sure," I reply, as Sharon pulls her brush from her

handbag and starts sprucing herself up for lunch with the boss. Amazing the difference it makes to your life if you're pretty, delicate and alluring like Sharon is. I see the guys rushing to open doors for her and help her if she has anything heavy to carry. Me? Nope - I'm left to struggle along with my arms full - bashing doors open with my enormous arse while men stand by, ogling at women like Sharon.

"See you later," she squeaks, wiggling her way out of the office and leaving me to my planning.

Within about 20 minutes, I've sent off about eight emails to newspapers and TV stations telling them of the plans to bring Christmas to the store, and I've been through dozens of leaflets and compiled a list of all the costs involved in my Christmas extravaganza, and how it will work. All I need to do now is wait for Keith to come back so I can run through them with him, then we'll be up and running.

As I'm waiting, a man puts his head round the door.

"Are you the manager?" he asks.

"Well, um. Yes!" I say. My claim to be running the place might be more convincing if I weren't covered in tinsel, but he doesn't seem unduly worried.

"Great. I want to buy a Christmas tree and arrange for it to be delivered."

"OK, well any of the guys in the gardening section can do that for you," I say. "Would you like me to take you there?"

"No, it's a bit more complicated than that. Do you mind if I come in?"

"Sure," I say, sitting back in my chair and luxuriating in this moment of executive power. "How can I help you?"

"Well the Christmas tree is to be delivered to someone famous," he says.

'*Oh, how exciting!*' I want to say...but I don't. I'm not *that* unprofessional. I do feel my eyebrows raise and my mouth open involuntarily though. I don't suppose my wide-eyed look is screaming 'I'm an executive', but there you go.

"OK," I say. "We service lots of famous people (we don't, no one famous has ever set foot in this place), so that won't be a problem, who is the Christmas tree for?"

"It's for David and Victoria Beckham," says the man. "So this would need to be handled with the utmost discretion."

Victoria Beckham. Victoria bloody Beckham.

"Discretion is our middle name here at Fosters," I say. "You can rest assured that we will deliver the best Christmas tree to the Beckhams, and to do so with every courtesy known to man."

"Good. OK. The next question is - what's the biggest tree you can get for me?"

"Have you seen the trees we've got outside?" I say. They all seem pretty bloody big to me.

"Those out there? No, no. They are nowhere near big enough. Can you show me some that are bigger?"

In the pile of booklets I've been looking through looking for costs is one from 'The Christmas Tree Company', I pull it out and show the man how big the Christmas trees can be. There is one that so massive it looks like it belongs in a pine forest.

"That's the sort of thing," he says.

"That is really massive though," I say. "Are you sure they want it to be that big?"

"Yes – absolutely sure," says the man. "They are having a huge Christmas party at their mansion and they need the entrance hall to look the open sequence of every Hollywood Christmas movie you've ever seen. If you can produce Frank Sinatra and have him coming down the stairs while crooning, that would be ideal."

He laughs at his own joke, but I have no idea who Frank Sinatra is so I just smile and shrug.

"The tree is £350."

"I'll pay now," he replies. "It needs to be delivered tomorrow."

"OK, I think delivery might be an extra charge. Can I call you when my assistant comes back and I'll confirm all the details and take the payment over the phone?"

I don't want to go much further here without running it all past Keith…I don't even know how we'd get hold of one of these enormous trees and I've no idea how we'd deliver it.

"Okay," says the man, standing up. "Let's do that, but do call as soon as you know. I want to get this sorted today."

"Let me take your name and number, and the details of the tree you want."

"Sure, my name's Mark Hutton," he says. He's just giving me his number when Keith comes thundering into the room on the wrong side of about four pints. Sharon is in his wake, giggling and red faced.

"Ah, is this your assistant?' asks Mark.

"Yes," I say, as Keith looks at me quizzically.

"Oh, I'm your assistant now, am I?" he asks.

"Yes, you are. Now Keith - this is Mark Hutton - he is here to buy a huge Christmas tree for Victoria and David Beckham. He wants to order it and get it delivered tomorrow. He wants one of these absolutely huge ones." I indicate the tree that he has chosen in the brochure.

Keith knows an exciting opportunity when he sees one, so he stops worrying about the fact that I described him as my assistant and gets on with the job of writing down the code for the tree that Mark has chosen. Within minutes he is placing the order.

"The delivery charge will be an additional £10," he says.

"Sure," says Mark. "That's fine - money isn't an issue. I just need to get everything organised." He looks down at the bunch of leaflets I've been looking through. "Do they have tree dressers in there?" he asks.

Tree dressers? Really? Do such people exist?

"What would be great would be if you could bring the tree and dress it at the house. Do you have someone who dresses trees?"

"I could do that," I say. "I'm in charge of Christmas."

A silence descends on the room. It's almost as if everyone present thinks that this is a disastrous idea.

"There would be a tight brief and it would have to be tastefully done," says Mark. "The Christmas party attracts the most important and glamorous people in the world."

"Absolutely. No problem at all. 'Tasteful' is my middle name," I respond, subconsciously touching the giant earrings and metres of tinsel strewn through my hair.

"OK, then we have a deal," says Mark, offering his hand. I shake it firmly and look over at Keith who looks quite terrified.

"I'll just put your bill together," says Keith, scratching his head and flicking through the brochures in front of him in a manner which suggests that he has no idea what to charge the Beckhams for the tree decorating service I've just offered. Once Mark has left, we all sit back and ponder what just happened.

"How much did you charge him for me?" I ask.

"£200," he says. "So I hope you're good at this sort of thing."

"I've no idea: I've never done anything like this in my life before. Mum and dad would never let me near the tree at home incase I ruined it."

CHAPTER FOUR

DAY WITH THE BECKHAMS

"You can't do that," says Ted, rather unsupportively, if you ask me.

"How hard can it be? I mean - really? How hard?"

"Really bloody hard," insists Ted. "People do proper university degrees in things like this."

"What? In dressing a Christmas tree? What are you talking about?"

"OK, maybe not dressing a tree, but - you know - home decor and making the place look good. Isn't it normally those guys - the interior designers - who do up trees and stuff and do party decorations and make everything look good?"

"I don't know," I say. "All I know is that I've had the brief from the party planning company and I've been googling 'how to decorate a tree' and I can't see that I'll have any problem at all, so please be more supportive."

Ted and I raise our glasses...me full of optimism and excitement, him full of dubiousness and concern.

. . .

NEIL PICKS me up at 8am the next morning and I'm dressed and ready to go. I washed my uniform last night and have ironed it. I'm wearing it with just a simple, white shirt underneath and I have done my make-up in an unobtrusive, elegant way. No tinsel, no stupid earrings, no madness at all. I'm all over this. No one needs to worry. Mary's got it all under control.

"We need to go to a shop to buy the stuff to go on the tree first," I say, directing Neil towards a boutique Christmas shop in Wimbledon, in which we have identified very posh decorations that will be perfect for the Beckhams' tree. I'm aware that I will have to reign myself in here, because my inclination is towards the flamboyant and fabulous and I suspect that Posh and her friends will be all about white and cream and all that understated bollocks. In fact, I know they are because of the very detailed brief I received late last night.

"Here it is," I say, as we arrive outside the shop, and Neil makes it clear that he's staying in the van and wants nothing to do with the choosing part of the operation.

"I've just come to do the heavy lifting," he says.

"OK, I'll go and have a look." I jump down from the van's seat and waddle to the front door. You have to ring a bell to gain entry. How poncey is that? They are selling decorations for God's sake.

I survey the beautiful interior of the shop - it looks like a jewellers, with the baubles laid out like they are precious jewels. Nothing in the shop has prices on. I've been told not to worry about the cost, just to pick the best, most classy decorations, and I have Keith's work Amex card in my bag. I start to look through them...they are all lovely, some of the baubles are made from shells and are incredibly delicate (I swerve those - I'm the clumsiest person alive, I'll break them if I so much as breathe on them), others have some sort of expensive sheen. They all look nice, but none of them looks brilliant. Do you know what I mean? None of them really stands out, or will send the guests home from the Beckham's house full of envy. They just aren't right. They are expensive and elegant but they aren't Chrsitmassy. They are not right for a Christmas tree party.

"I need to think about this," I say to the lady in the shop, leaving and walking back to the van to talk to Neil. He sees me coming and winds down the window.

"Everything OK?"

"Yes," I say, "But the decorations are really plain. I don't think they're quite what I want."

"It's not about you though, doll face, it's about the Beckhams. They like all that sort of shit."

"I know. But I want to do something really special for them. Can you come in and help me?"

Neil has lit up a cigarette and clearly has no desire to leave the warmth and familiarity of his van to look for decorations.

"Mate, I know nothing about bloody decorations," he says. "I can't tell the difference between the posh ones and those ones there…" he points towards the cheap pound shop next to us, and I follow his pointed finger…and that's when I see them…the absolute best Christmas decorations you've ever seen - bright pink with cat's faces and whiskers on them.

"OH MY GOD. I love them," I squeal. "They are perfect!"

"What? Perfect for the Beckhams? Are you sure?"

"I've never been more sure of anything in my life," I say, running towards the shop as if drawn by a giant magnet.

It's so much better in this shop. Way less poncey than the other place and the decorations are so much nicer.

I buy 30 of the pink baubles with cat faces on, and some which are shaped like pigs. Pigs flying through the Christmas tree with little curly tails that move...who doesn't want to see that on a Christmas morning? I buy tonnes of tinsel because they have it in pink, and I know that posh is all about coordination. I've seen her in Heat magazine - everything she wears matches everything else. I have bags and bags of goodies at the end. Bags bursting with pinkness. This is going to be amazing.

Then, I have a sudden thought...why don't I get some of these for the shop as well? I pile even more into my baskets and stagger towards the cashier.

"Look at this little lot," I say to Neil when I get back to the van. He jumps out of his seat and looks stunned as he puts the dozen or so carrier bags into the van.

"Bloody brilliant, eh?" I say, but he just sort of half-smiles and asks me whether I'm really sure that pink Christmas baubles with cat faces on and pig shaped decorations are what's required.

Er...yes. They're perfect.

We drive along in companionable silence, into the countryside and in the direction of the Beckham's lovely country house. I can see the black wrought iron canopy in the distance, leading to the front door. It looks so familiar. I feel like I've been here before, but it's just all the research I did (mad googling last night) that has made the place look so familiar. I know that beneath that canopy lies a cream and black tiled path. I can't wait to see it all.

But when we pull up at the gates and ring the intercom, there are problems.

"It's impossible for you to come in," says a haughty voice. "We are having difficulties."

"Oh," says Neil. "We've come to deliver and decorate the Christmas tree. What would you like me to do with it?"

There's murmuring in the background and raised voices, then eventually the gates open and we pass through them and head up the driveway towards the house. I'm so excited. I can't wait until she sees the tree when it's all decked out. She's going to absolutely love it and the two of us will instantly become best friends and probably go on holiday every year with Ted and David.

Fantasies about David and I frollicking on a sun-drenched beach are bouncing through my mind as we pull up in front of the palatial abode and I waddle towards the door, preparing to wrap Victoria in a warm embrace. But there's no Posh Spice to greet me, just a large, Polish-sounding lady. She apologises profusely for not letting us in at the gate earlier.

"There was misunderstanding. Problems are here. Harper is bad girl today. Mr and Mrs Beckham are not happy. They are very upset."

"Oh I see," I say. "Sorry to hear that. Are we OK to come in now?"

"Yes, must come through," she says, ushering us both into a hallway that is every bit as spectacular as I hoped it would be. It has a wide staircase in the centre, featuring a large window on the landing half-way up which gives a wonderful view of their magnificent garden.

From a distant room I can hear the sounds of a young girl screaming and stamping her feet in a tantrum.

"You can go in there," says the Polish lady, pointing to a side room. Neil and I wander in, sheepishly, and are introduced to three party planners - all painfully thin, dressed in identical black outfits, and looking very sombre. It becomes clear that they are fed up because they wanted to be the ones dressing the tree. My arrival has come as something as a shock to them. They think that, because they are responsible for all the other aspects of the party, they should be responsible for dressing the tree so everything is coordinated.

What is also clear is that I have been billed as the ultimate

Christmas expert and the woman who will make the tree look amazing.

"I hear you've done this a million times before." says the tallest of the women. She has sleek brown hair styled in a razor-sharp bob and the shiniest, most pointy boots I've ever seen.

"Your boots are lovely," I say, quite mesmerised by them.

"Thank you," she replies, and I seem to have escaped without having to answer her question.

"Do you think you should tell them that you've never done anything like this before," whispers Neil. "I mean - look around you - everything is white and cream. There's no pink anywhere."

"Just relax," I say. "Don't worry about a thing."

While Neil and three gardeners go outside to bring the tree in, the party planners help me to bring in the bags of decorations. We put them all down in the hallway and I begin to unload the bags.

"Holy fucking Christ, are you joking?" says the older woman in the group. I think she's probably in charge. She is the prettiest, with lovely auburn tumbling curls and a perfect creamy complexion.

"How do you mean?"

"I mean...flying pigs? Flying pigs? Do you know who's coming tonight? Everyone from Elton John to the Home Secretary is going to be here."

"Yay! Elton's going to love the pigs. And the cats. Look at these," I say, pulling out the cat baubles while waving them around and meowing. "Great, aren't they?"

There's silence from the three women, all of whom are staring at me as if I've grown an extra pair of eyes.

"This is unimaginably horrific," said razor-sharp bob woman.

"No, it's not. They're lovely. Look," I said, wiggling the

pigs in the air and making 'oink oink' sounds. "It's going to be really lovely. I promise you."

"We're going to find Victoria," says the third woman. She's very tall and very thin with quite a harsh angular face. Her legs are so incredibly thin they look like they might snap.

Once the women have gone, we get the tree into place. I decide that there's no point waiting for them to return. I might as well get on with the decorations, so I climb up onto a step ladder and begin making it look fantastic...and - my God - it does. It looks brilliant by the time I've finished. It screams 'Christmas'. I have lined all the little pigs up so they are chasing each other round the tree. They all have lovely big snouts. Honestly, it's the best tree ever.

In the background I can hear the party planner women coming back. Posh is with them. She's much prettier than she looks on television. She has a real softness about her, and these enormous eyes. I decide I definitely want her to be my best friend.

"Oh my God, Oh my God," she says, her hands flying to her mouth as she looks at the tree.

See, I knew she'd love it.

I wonder whether she's spotted the giant pig on the top. (I forgot to get a star...I can't think of everything).

Then she starts shouting.

"This is the worst day of my life," she says. "It's all I need with Harper playing up all morning. Nothing will stop her crying. This is the worst Christmas ever. Can you all just get out of my house."

"Me?" I say, looking at her with incredulity. "You want me to go?"

"Yes," says Victoria. "Just go before I call security." The sound of Harper's wails fill the room. She sounds really distressed.

"Oh God, this is unbearable," says Posh. "I just can't stand this anymore - a screaming child and a ridiculous, cheap and nasty Christmas tree."

The three party planning women glare at me as she speaks.

"But it's lovely," I try. "It's different and fun and..."

As I speak, Harper stomps in, tears streaming down her face and anger and frustration written into every pore. Then she looks up, sees the tree, and is mesmerised.

"Ooooooo," she coos. "It's so lovely. Is it for me?"

She has finally stopped crying. She wipes away the last of the tears as she stares up at the tree, delight replacing the sadness on her face. Then she smiles the most enormous smile. "It's the best thing I've ever seen in my life. Thank you mummy."

Harper throws herself into her mother's arms, then takes Posh by the hand and leads her to examine the tree carefully. "See the piggies," she squeals.

Posh turns round and smiles at me. "Thank you," she mouths, as the party planners almost faint from the shock of it all. "You're a star. This is amazing."

A clear victory, I'm sure you'll agree, for the fat girl and her gaudy candyfloss pink decorations against the very skinny ladies in black.

CHAPTER FIVE

*I*t's 4pm and the great story of my success at the Beckhams' house this morning is spreading through the store like a bushfire. There have been mixed reactions to the news that the Beckhams loved my interior designing skills. Actually, no - that's not true - scrub that! The reactions have all been the same - everyone is GOB-SMACKED. They just can't believe that I could have made such a success of it.

"I'm really pleased for you, but AMAZED," says Sharon, while Neil regales everyone with the details.

"The look on the stylists' face was a picture," he's saying. "They were all there, dressed head-to-toe in some fancy designer gear, and up rocks Mary in her bloody green over-alls which make her look like Kermit the frog, and she's twice the size of all of them put together."

"Alright, alright," I say. "No need to get personal."

"Sorry, love, but it was very, very funny."

I can see that some of the women in the group are wild with jealousy that I managed to pull it off..I got myself inside the Beckham's house and decorated a Christmas tree in a manner that delighted them. I know that half the people here today were really hoping I'd mess up...I am determined to rub my victory in as much as I can.

"Call me Kelly Hoppen!" I keep saying. "I'm the queen of interior design."

We're all gathered in the giant gardening conservatory in front of the company Christmas trees that I have done out in the style of Posh's tree. We're going to trade off the link to the Beckhams to sell as many of these trees as possible. There is a whole row of them, all with the little pigs chasing each other across them, and lovely pink cat faces looking out. They are heavily bedecked with tons of tinsel that I have just thrown onto them, like I did with Victoria Beckham's, to create a look that is both artistic and spontaneous. In short, my trees look completely amazing.

Sharon isn't convinced. "What was it about the tree that the Beckhams loved so much," she asks."I mean - I'm not being funny but you wouldn't imagine Victoria thinking that it was very sophisticated."

"She did," I reply quickly. "She thought the tree was stylish and elegant and leant a certain stylish flavour to the house. I'm lying, of course. I'm not going to mention to anyone that I only got away with it because of the intervention of a small child.

Sharon nods, disbelievingly, and continues to stare at my mad, pink trees.

To be honest, the whole shop looks stunning today, following the implementation of my Christmas plans. You should see the nativity scene - a large area in the corner of the store filled with hay and a wild flashing neon shining star. There's a giant stuffed donkey and dolls representing the main biblical characters. It's truly outstanding. It's just a shame that the stuffed donkey is twice the size of Joseph, but it's impossible to get life-sized characters, and - believe me -

I've looked everywhere. So the donkey is looming over everyone in a slightly threatening way. He's also wobbly on his legs, so I've had to lean him up against the manger which does nothing to diminish his intimidating presence in the scene.

Away from the nativity, there's a beautiful area for Father Christmas to sit and meet children - it's full of fake snow and sleighs and has Christmas music playing and the occasional jingle-jangle of sleigh bells. There are also elves and a couple of fairies (I liked them - I know they're not in the original tale, but they look really cute).

Then there's the pile of presents for Santa to hand to children and the sweets and cards I've bought...it all looks great.

"Blimey, how much did this lot cost?" asks Keith. "Did you really get it all for under £200?"

"Yes, of course," I say (no I didn't – it was nearer £500).

"Well done," he says. "Well done, indeed. This is all amazing."

As we are talking, Mandy from accounts walks across the gardening section towards me, holding the most beautiful bunch of pink flowers I've ever seen in my life. It's an enormous bouquet. She hands it to me, and I lean over and give Keith kiss on the cheek to thank him for them.

"What the hell are you doing, woman?" he says.

"I'm thanking you for these flowers," I say, beginning to open the envelope tucked into them.

"I didn't get you those. Why on earth would I buy you flowers?"

"Because I went to the Beckhams this morning and did their tree and because I made the shop look amazing," I say, then I read out what's written on the card:

"Thank you so much for making our Christmas tree look wonderful. You are a superstar, much love, Victoria and David Beckham x."

"Yay! Have you seen this?" I say to Keith, showing him the card.

"Bloody hell!" he says, genuinely impressed with what he's seeing. "I don't believe you've just had flowers from David Beckham."

"David Beckham? Really? Has David Beckham sent you flowers?" a young mother comes up to me, having overheard Keith's words. She's at the nativity scene with her son and declares herself a huge fan of the former footballer. "Can I see the card?" she asks.

"Yes, of course," I reply, proudly, showing the greeting, buried in the floral arrangement, and watching her swoon before me.

Quite a crowd has gathered around me, as people regard my flowers admiringly.

"Why has he sent flowers?" asks one man, smartly-dressed and a little out of place among the pink trees, tinsel and toddlers.

"I went over and decorated his Christmas tree, just like that one," I say, pointing towards the large tree in front of us."That's a replica of the Beckhams' Christmas tree."

A lady pulls her phone out and takes pictures of the tree. She's soon joined by others, all flashing away and capturing the image of my pink, glittery tree in their phones.

"Would you stand next to it," asks one lady, then it feels like dozens of people are taking pictures.

You can hear the hum of general chatter in the store, punctuated with 'David Beckham...Victoria Beckham...pink tree...' as they share the information and post their news to Twitter and Facebook.

"Are you available to come and decorate my tree?" asks one lady.

"Oh yes!" says another.

Then there are lots of questions about where I got the

decorations from, and whether they will be on sale in the store, and I'm filled with a warm glow and a rush of excitement at the thought that flying pigs in Christmas trees are going to be ALL the rage in this affluent part of Surrey this festive period.

"We need to capitalise on this," says Keith. "I'm going to get onto the warehouse and order loads of decorations like these and we'll sell them in the store. I'll make a sign: '*You too could have a Christmas tree like David Beckham.*' You're a bloody genius, Mary. Really, you are."

"That's a great idea," I say. "We could sell loads and get some of the money back that I spent on this place."

"It was only £200, don't worry about it," says Keith.

"Have you got a minute?" someone says to me. I turn around to see a small woman standing there.

"Of course. How can I help?"

"I'm from the Cobham Advertiser, I'm just here shopping but I couldn't help overhearing what you said. Is there any chance I could do an interview with you?"

"Yes," I say. "Of course."

There's another woman behind her, she's just arrived and is on her phone but signalling that she needs to talk to me.

"Hi, I work on Vogue magazine. I saw the trees on Twitter. We'd really like to do a shoot in here. Would that be possible? We'd bring models in and put them around the Beckham Tree for a feature online."

"Hi, sorry - but I was here first. The interview will only take about 10 or 15 minutes, then we can get the story of online in the next couple of hours, and it will be in the paper at the end of the week," she says. "The Cobham Advertiser, your local paper. Good for sales."

"Sure. Absolutely fine," I say.

"And do you mind if I get my photographer to come?"

"No problem," I say. I look around and see Keith standing there with his thumb up.

"So, that's OK?" says the woman from Vogue.

"Yes," I say.

"Well done, sweetheart," says Keith. "You go off and do the interview, and we'll talk later. Remember the party tonight - it's going to be rocking."

"Sure," I say. Works' Christmas party...rocking...Great!

CHAPTER SIX

THE OFFICE CHRISTMAS PARTY

"*W*hy are they holding the party in such an odd place," says Ted. To get the work Christmas party we have to drive over this complicated road system. "Keep your eyes peeled," he says (isn't that a horrible image...like someone's taken your eyeballs out and is skinning them with a vegetable peeler).

The junction in Hounslow reminds me of when you go over that bridge to get into Wales. Do you know the one I mean? Is there any more fun to be had in the world than when you go over that, then suddenly there are no lanes, and it's a mad free-for-all to get into a lane when they arrive. I love it. Ted and I went away for the weekend to Cardiff and went over that bridge and we were both screaming as he drove flat out on the road with no lane markings at all, fighting against all the other traffic to get to the front of the lanes when they arrived.

"Can we go back and do it again?" he asked. He said it was worth £6 just for the sheer thrill. Cheaper than Thorpe Park and *so* much more enjoyable.

Anyway - I'm only telling you about our day out in Wales

because this bloody road system is just as bad...it's like wacky races, with cars shooting around us from every direction.

"Left," I say. I'm in charge of map reading but I can't make head nor tail of the map or the roads (two crucial things that you absolutely need to be able to make head and tail of in order to have a fighting chance of offering even half decent directions).

We finally find the place - it's a big hotel called 'The Fallgate'. Ted pulls over and I jump out. He's not coming with me tonight because it's a 'no partners' party. They do this so that we are forced to mingle and can't just sit there chatting to the person we came with all evening. It just means being stuck in a corner talking to Jed from the lighting department about bulbs and lampshades.

"I wish you were coming," I say to Ted, as he kisses me goodbye.

"You'll have more fun without me," he replies. "Anyway - I've got the football to watch. Call me later, OK?"

"OK," I say, as I watch him drive off, waving through the open window as he goes. I do love that man, you know. He drives me nuts sometimes but he means everything.

I pull out my phone and text Neil to see if he's here...I don't fancy walking into the room on my own and having to frantically scan faces, looking for someone I know. On my phone there are about 20 missed calls and a whole stack of messages. Christ. Every journalist in London is keen to talk to me about my experience at the Beckhams. The Cobham Advertiser interview must have gone online...now everyone knows about my Christmas tree experiences. It's like I'm famous or something. I'm not quite sure what to do, so I tuck my phone back into my bag and decide to sort it out tomorrow. Right now I need a large drink and a large handful of salted, savoury snacks.

In the main foyer of the hotel there's a sign:

"The Felgate is pleased to welcome all the staff of Fosters DIY stores in the north Surrey area. We hope you have a lovely evening and a very Happy Christmas."

Excellent, That's nice. Except that the sign doesn't say where we have to go. It's nice to get a cheery festive greeting, but some directions would also be nice.

I wander through the reception area, looking for clues. There's no reply from Neil and I have forgotten to bring my invitation with me, telling me which room to go to, so I walk slowly through the marble reception area hoping to bump into someone I know. Just in front of me is a group of three people - all fat, middle aged, and waddling through towards the Queen Anne Room.

Perfect. They look exactly like employees from Fosters and - yes - Queen Anne room rings a bell. I follow them into the room and help myself to a glass of wine from the guy on the door. The wine is lovely...really expensive-tasting stuff. I sip at it while I wander round looking for my work colleagues, but there are so many people here it's extremely hard to find them. A guy walks past with a tray of the lovely wine, so I take another one, putting my empty glass on his tray. I'm so impressed that they have done this party properly, with a beautiful, big elegant room featuring a large Christmas tree, but I'm disappointed that I haven't been asked to dress it. Great to have proper, good quality wine and not the normal cheap rubbish that gets served. I might have another one. Still no sign of anyone I know though.

"Very posh, isn't it?" I say to the couple next to me. "And everyone looks very swanky out of their green overalls, don't they?"

They look at me in the same way that one might look at an axe murderer, running down the street towards you, clutching a sharpened blade. They back off and turn to talk to someone else.

"Right - ladies and gentleman," says a toastmaster, resplendent in a uniform of red waistcoat and black frock coat, banging a hammer down to get everyone's attention. "Welcome to the Christmas dinner and drinks for Parker & Parker Legal services. Please move down through the reception room into the main dining hall where dinner will be served."

Shit. I'm in the wrong bloody party.

"Please go through," says the toastmaster, signalling towards the dining area. I have to admit I'm tempted just to stay in this party. They don't look as if they're short of a bob or two. I bet the food will be lovely - much nicer than the naff bits of pastry that will no doubt be served at our shin-dig.

"I just need to pop out to make a call," I say, moving towards the front doors of the room.

"Of course," says the toastmaster, opening the door and allowing me to go through. As I leave, I help myself to another glass of wine from a tray on the side. Once I'm outside I check my phone.

"It's the Queen Maryl room," says the text from Neil. Bollocks. Queen Mary, not Queen Anne.

I get to the right place, and it's much more like I imagined it would be; plain and tired looking with a simple pay bar in the corner...no elaborate decorations, no toastmaster and no delicious free wine.

"Here's to Parker & Parker," I say, raising my glass, and promising myself that if I ever need any legal work doing, they will be the firm I turn to before any other.

"OK, ladies and gentlemen," says Keith, taking the microphone and looking for all the world like a low-rent comedian on a cruise ship. "Let's get this party starteeeed."

There are a few feeble claps from those who have bothered to gather in front of him. The rest of us just mill around, waiting for what will be an overlong and under-prepared speech.

"Hey, gather round," he shouts over to us. "We're really partying over here."

"There you are, hero of the hour," says Neil, throwing a cursory Christmas decoration at me for no good reason. "We'd better go over there and pretend to like the boss."

Keith's eyes light up when he sees us coming towards him. He's a nice guy really. He's been a good boss to me over the couple of years that I've been at the company. He's just a bit...I don't know - a bit naff, I suppose. Gosh that sounds harsh, but do you know what I mean? He's just a bit too much like David Brent from The Office for anyone to take him seriously.

"We're going to do a fun quiz," he announces.

Those of us gathered before him do nothing to disguise our distaste. Fun and quiz are not words that have any right to be snuggling up to one another in the same sentence.

Keith divides us into four teams of five people and invites us to get a chair each and congregate in our newly-formed groups, so the fun can begin. Since trying to organise 20 people when most of them are drunk is a little like trying to herd cats, this process takes about 20 minutes, and by the time we're all finally sitting down and ready to start, I, for one, am losing the will to live. Keith looks more exasperated than any man has ever looked before.

"Finally," he says. "Right - now for the quiz...can you nominate a person in each group to write down the answers."

Again, given the level of alcohol consumption, this takes way, way longer than it has any right to.

"Come on," says Keith. "It's like trying to get toddlers to organise themselves."

It strikes me that this is a pretty good analogy. Drunk people are very much like toddlers...staggering into things, unable to make it to the toilet on time, and babbling nonsensically.

Finally, *finally*, we are in our groups and have appointed a leader and Keith can start his God-forsaken, entirely unwelcome, quiz.

"OK," he says. "In the store, we asked questions of lots of people and I have the answers here. You have to guess what they said. The person who gets closest wins the prize. Does that make sense?"

"Yes," we all chorus, hoping there aren't too many of them.

"OK, ready for the first question?"

"Yes," we all say again, with slightly less enthusiasm. I wish he'd just get on with the damn thing.

"OK. What is the worst way to start your day?" he asks. "Would the appointed spokesperson in each team please raise their hand when they are ready."

I throw my arm into the air before even consulting with the team. Sandra from the catering department voices her anger.

"Well, do you have an answer?" I ask her, she mutters that she doesn't, so I turn back towards Keith, waving my arm impatiently.

"OK, Mary's hand was up first. What do you think the answer is?"

"Is the answer: the worst way to start your day is to wake up on the floor and discover that your Siamese twin is missing...the one with the vital internal organs. Is that the answer?"

"No, Mary. No," says Keith, looking distressed.

"OK - in a prison cell."

Everyone looks open-mouthed. Well, what did they expect? This is supposed to be the worst way to start your day. It's got to be something bad.

"Dead," I say. "Is that the answer? Worse way you can wake up is dead."

"No."

Turns out the right answer is "having overslept" - for God's sake. That's really not the worst way to start your day...I can think of loads of worst ways.

"Mary, you have a peculiar imagination," says Simon from customer services. "Remind me never to be left alone with you on a dark night."

"Next question," says Keith. "Let's see if someone other than Mary can answer. Mary - please make your answers less...what's the word I'm looking for?...troubling."

"OK," I mutter, but I'm not put off, I'm in my stride now, and determine that we should win this game.

"And let the others on your team contribute," he adds. "It's a team quiz." .

"Yes," I say, but I'm thinking '*fuck that...I've got a load of dimwits on my team.*'

We play for the next hour. HOUR! At a bloody Christmas party. On several occasions I contemplate leaving and going back to that lovely lawyers' party. That was so much more classy, and no one was asking stupid questions, and judging you on your answers.

"OK, this one is the decider," says Keith, now clearly losing patience with us, and losing confidence in his own game. "The question is - what was the name of my childhood friend?"

Marty from the kitchen department throws his hand into the air immediately. He's an odd-looking creature is Marty - he's extremely thin, skeletal really, he kind of looks like a box of KFC after you've eaten all the chicken and thrown the bones back in. He's also a terrible chain smoker in a real old-school way. He smokes roll-ups and has the yellow fingers to prove it.

"Was your friend called Mike?" he asks.

"No," says Keith.

"Barry?"

"No"

"Peter?"

"No, look Marty - you can't just keep shouting out names, you have to confer with your team and come up with an answer between you. "Anyone else?"

"I know," I say. "Did you not have any friends? Maybe you just had an old cereal box which you painted a face onto and called it Brian the box, and that became your best friend?"

Keith looks at me as if I'm the most ridiculous person on earth.

"Let's end the quiz there. Everyone has won," he says. "Collect your free drink from the bar whenever you're ready."

It strikes me that this is not the best quiz prize ever, since there's a free bar running between 9 and 10pm, but I don't want to bring this up with Keith. I've clearly upset him somehow...he's staring at me like I'm some sort of lunatic. Does he need to be reminded that I'm actually nearly famous?

Behind me Father Christmas is saying his 'ho, ho, hos' and swigging from a bottle of beer.

"Alright?" asks Neil.

"I'm fine," I say. "I'm just admiring Father Christmas. He's a bloody handsome fella."

"I'm going to make a bet with you, Mary bloody Brown. Yes - we're going to have a bloody bet, you and me...a bloody bet."

"OK," I say, ordering myself a bottle of wine (the free bar's only there for an hour, I need to fill my boots while I can). "Go on then, let's have a bet."

CHAPTER SEVEN

A DAY OFF

*T*hank Christ I haven't got to go to work today...I took the day off to do my Christmas shopping and it turns out it was the best decision in the world: I don't think I've ever felt so bad.

I stretch out in bed and feel immediately constrained by something. I can't fathom what it is, but it's really bloody annoying. I look over to see that I'm fully dressed and my sleeve is caught on the bedstead. Strangely, I appear to be dressed as Father Christmas. Ow - and my leg really hurts. Whichever way you look at it, this is not good. Questions which immediately spring to mind are: where are my real clothes? What did Father Christmas go home wearing, since I appear to have his outfit? At what stage did Father Christmas and I swap clothes, and did I do this publicly? And why does my leg hurt so much? I think Sharon, my new best friend, might be the person to ask.

I pick up the phone gingerly and dial her number. She answers straight away with a girlish chuckle.

"Mary Brown. What are you like?" she says.

I don't know," I want to reply. "What am I like? Tell me."

"So you got home safely then?" she asks, laughing again, clearly at some memory of me that she is not choosing to share.

"Home safely," I say. "All dressed as Father Christmas…"

"Ha," she laughs, giving nothing away.

"I was surprised to wake up in a Santa costume," I say, hopeful that she'll explain my outfit to me.

"Well, you took the bet," she says.

"Yes, indeed."

What bet? What's she talking about? I don't think Sharon hangs around too many people who get hideously drunk, or she'd know with absolute certainty that she needs to spell these things out to me or I won't know what on earth is going on.

"Well, I'd better go," she says. "It's crazy, crazy here today. The store's packed thanks to you…people are queuing to get into the car park. Father Christmas is booked up until 9pm on Christmas Eve. It's totally mad. Keith says people are driving hundreds of miles to see the Beckham Tree and to buy the decorations, and there are loads and loads of journalists wanting to talk to you. They are all coming in tomorrow. I hope that's OK?"

"Of course," I say.

"Bye," she says, and she disappears off the line, leaving me none the wiser about the bloody outfit I'm wearing and some bet I had.

I text Neil. "Did I make some sort of bet last night?" I ask him. A couple of minutes later, the phone rings and all I can hear is Neil guffawing and chortling. So, that'll be a 'yes' then.

"Just stop laughing and tell me what I did," I say.

"Do you really not remember?"

"Not a thing," I say.

"You had a bet with Dom and Pete from the warehouse

that you could get yourself onto *This Morning*, the TV show. The bet was that you have to wear that Father Christmas costume until you've been on there."

"Been on there?"

"Yeah - you either have to be mentioned by them, be on the phone to them...on air, or go on to the show, but since you have to wear the Father Christmas costume all the time you might not want to do that."

Oh, for God's sake.

"That's a ridiculous bet. There's no way I can do that. Why did I end up doing a bet with them?"

"Because you were drunk?"

"Well, yes, that's hard to deny. How long have I got in which to get myself onto *This Morning*?" I ask.

"As long as you like," says Neil. "But you have to wear the Father Christmas costume until you've been on there, so I wouldn't leave it too long."

Oh ffs.

Now, if I were a sensible, rational grown-up, I'd take the Father Christmas outfit off at this stage, fold it up and put it to one side and dismiss the whole thing as a drunken prank at a Christmas party, but I'm not like that. I've got this maverick streak in me, and once I say I'm going to do something, I make sure I damn well do it. Or, certainly, I give it a try. This one might be beyond even me, though. Get onto This Morning? With lovely Holly and Phil Schofield? Bloody hell.

I make myself a cup of tea and take a banana (I curse my bloody diet on days like this...no one wants to be eating fruit when they're hung-over, bacon was invented for the very purpose of comforting drinkers the morning after).

I sit down, peel the banana and switch the television on to ITV. As I do, my phone bleeps with a message. I take a look:

"Thank you for your order from Top Shop. Your parcel will be dispatched from our depot today."

What order?

I go through my emails and find one entitled 'order confirmation'. In fact, scrub that - I find three entitled 'order confirmation' - one from Topshop for three dresses (all size 10, I would be a size 20 in Top Shop clothes if they did clothes in my size), one from River Island for a pair of shoes size 8 (I'm size 5) and one for underwear from Agent Provocateur that would shame a pole dancer. Nipple less? Really? Where the hell was my mind last night? Can it be true that I sat down at my computer at midnight, dressed as Father Christmas, drunk out of my mind, and ordered 'peep panties' and 'nippleless bras'? Yes, apparently, it is.

I'm never drinking again. Never. Not ever.

There are also loads of emails from journalists wanting to interview me. I'll have to get back to them all later. My life's just a little bit out of control at the moment.

On *This Morning*, Phil and Holly are looking very serious. The beautiful Holly with her perfect hair and lovely face is doing puppy eyes into the camera lens. "If you have been affected by drugs in any way, call in now and talk to our experts."

OK. This has to be my moment. I've never seen drugs, heard anything about drugs and I don't know anyone who's on drugs, but still - I pick up my landline and dial the number. I have to get myself mentioned on *This Morning*.

"*This Morning*, Annabel speaking."

"Hi, I was just ringing about the drugs," I say.

"Of course, how can I help you?"

"I'm addicted to drugs," I say, biting into my banana. "I'd like to talk to Holly and Phil about it...on air."

"Certainly. Can you tell me a little about your problems..."

"I've always had them," I begin. "Since I was a child."

"A child, really? So, how old were you when you first started taking drugs?"

I can sense that the child angle is a good one, and she's interested in me because I took drugs when I was young.

"I first took drugs when I was four," I say, thinking that will pique her interest.

"When you were four? Really? Gosh, that's young."

Yep - interest is officially piqued.

"How were you introduced to them? I mean - where does a four-year-old come across drugs?"

"Mum," I say, and there's a short silence.

"That must have been really tough," she says. "Your mum was an addict?"

"She was," I say. "She made me take them."

"OK, look, we're going to put you on air in three minutes, is that OK?"

"Yes," I say, grabbing my mobile to text the guys at work. They won't bloody believe this.

"I'm on This Morning in three minutes!!" I text.

"So, welcome Mary. Can you hear me? Also, Mary - can I ask you to turn your mobile phone off - we're getting some feedback here from it."

Lovely Holly is talking to me! It's so exciting. "Of course, just doing that now" I reply, switching my mobile off, but already I can see Neil's reply is a whole load of smiley faces and the message 'am watching it now'. .

"Would you tell us briefly what happened to you? Is it true that your mother forced you on to drugs, Mary?"

"Yes, it is," I say. "When I was four-years-old she started feeding me drugs and I became hooked on them."

"That's terrible. We're joined by Dr Mike in the studio. Is there anything you'd like to ask him?"

The truth is that there's nothing I want to ask anyone,

and I don't want to take up too much of their time in case there's someone waiting with real issues to discuss. All I want to do is make sure that everyone at work knows I'm on the show.

"I just want to say how difficult it is," I say. "And I want to urge mothers everywhere never to give drugs to their children because it ruins lives. My name's Mary Brown and my life has been ruined by them."

"Indeed," says Holly, turning to the doctor in the studio to talk about my entirely fabricated life story. "How hard for Mary. Is that something that anyone can ever come to terms with?"

The doctor explains that I need counselling and drugs therapy and I'm urged to stay on the line so they can talk to me afterwards to offer me the help that I need.

"Thanks, I'm OK," I tell the producer and I put the phone down, stand up and remove the blasted Father Christmas costume.

"Victory!" I say, laughing to myself. "A lovely little victory."

CHAPTER EIGHT

CHRISTMAS SHOPPING

I'm not feeling overwhelmingly proud of myself as I grab my handbag, put on some lipstick and push the front-door open. Phoning a national television station and pretending to be on drugs isn't ideal behaviour... Oh well, no one will know it was me and at least I won the daft bet. Dishy Dave who lives just below me is leaving his flat as I step out.

"Ah, glad to see you're up and about," he says. "I didn't think you'd be leaving your bed today."

"Why wouldn't I be up and about?" I reply. "I have Christmas shopping to do."

"Well, mainly I thought you wouldn't be up today because of the state you were in last night. Don't you remember falling down and me helping you up. I'm surprised you don't have a bruise on your leg. You took a nasty fall."

"Oh," I reply, pleased to know where the painful bruise came from, but a bit embarrassed that Dave saw me.

"You were all dressed up," he continues.

"Yes, that's right - Christmas party. Now I better get on my way, I've got Christmas shopping to do."

"You said last night that you were planning to do all your shopping on Amazon."

Christ - how long did I talk to him for last night?

"I changed my mind," I say, bluntly. "See you later."

I offer a cheery wave as I step out onto the pavement. I had planned to do all my shopping online, my drunk self was right about that, and the last thing I want to do with a bloody hangover is go shopping, but online shopping is not a great way to buy the right presents, and I got fed up of ordering things then when they turned up, finding they weren't quite right, and having to send them back.

I also got really fed up of all these advertising emails... I bought mum a book about woodland birds, and got an email saying "if you liked the book about woodland birds, perhaps you'd like these..." There followed a whole selection of things like tea cosies, screwdriver kits, and children's Postman Pat dressing up outfits. On what planet does buying a book about birds for your mum mean that you are secretly hankering after a Postman Pat costume?

The first shop I come across on the High Street is Argos. In common with everyone else in the world, I've no idea why the shop is still going, or, indeed, how it ever started in the first place. Still, I go in there, and wander around, thinking how utterly bizarre it is. I flick through the catalogue and my eye is caught by a painting set. My mum has always wanted to learn to paint...this would be perfect... There is a mini easel, paints and pads as well as brushes and all the other paraphernalia of introductory-level painting. It really would be absolutely perfect. My dad always rings me before Christmas to ask what he should get mum, this year I told him to book her a painting course, so when I arrive with this on Christmas morning, it will complete the package. She'll be delighted, and me and dad will look like superheroes.

So I take out a piece of paper, write the number of the

item onto it with the tiny, little pen,, and take the piece of paper to the desk. This is where shopping in Argos becomes a bit like battleships, trying to work out from this side of the wall what's on the other side of the wall.

It turns out that they do have the painting set. Bull's-eye! So I pay my money and wait in line, under a blue light on the far side of the room, looking up at the screen, like I'm waiting for train details to emerge on the phalanx of screens at Waterloo station.

The art set arrives, and I head off feeling very proud of myself that mum's present has been bought. I think how happy she'll be when I give it to her on Christmas Day. But as soon as I start thinking about Christmas, I start thinking about the whole issue of the fact that I still haven't talked to Ted properly about what we're going to do. I really need to have a chat with him about the fact that I have accepted two lunch invitations and we need to go to both, but the time never seems right.

I wander into Marks and Spencer on the way through the centre, just to see whether there's anything in there that would be nice for dad this Christmas.

A lady walks up to the shop assistant in front of me.

"May I try on that dress in the window please?" she asks.

"Certainly not madam," I find myself saying. "You have to use the fitting room like everyone else."

OK, so it was funnier in my head than it was when I said it out loud, but - it's Christmas - time for having fun and not taking everything too seriously.

The woman scowls at me, as if I've just trodden on her cat, or kicked her baby, or something, while I offer a reluctant smile and shuffle away.

So, back to the big question of the day - what the hell should I get dad for Christmas? I mean - what does anyone get their father for Christmas? It's the stupidest present in the world to buy. If I get socks or a tie or cufflinks, he won't be remotely impressed - he just has absolutely no interest in that sort of thing. But what else do I get?

I pull my phone out of my bag to ring Charlie and see whether she has any thoughts. It's switched off, which strikes me as odd. I'm the sort of person who has my phone on all day and all night. I think I'd have to go for counselling if I ever lost it. I never switch it off. NEVER. It's so odd that it's not on.

Then I remember that lovely Holly told me to switch it off while we were filing The Morning. I switch it back on and phone Charlie.

"Hiya gorgeous," I say.

"At last," she replies. "Why haven't you returned any of my messages?"

"Sorry - my phone was off in my bag, I didn't see that I had any. What's so urgent?"

"What's so urgent? Fuck me, Mary - you were on national television this morning telling the world that your mum pushed drugs on you. Your mum is frantic and is ringing me to find out what the hell is going on. What were you thinking?"

"Oh that!" I say. "Don't worry about that - it was just a bet I had with one of the guys in the office. Nothing to worry about."

"Yes - lots to worry about, Mary. You're mum's going loopy. You have to ring her. Call her now then ring me straight back."

"OK," I say. I just didn't think that anyone would twig that it was me on the television this morning...perhaps I should have given a false name, but Mary Brown is such a common name, there didn't seem to be any point.

I dial mum's number and prepare myself to get screamed

at. But it's a rather quiet, subdued mum who answers the phone.

"Why did you say those things?" she asks, pitifully. "I don't understand."

I explain about the bet and me being an idiot and not thinking it through.

"I'm so sorry mum," I say, when I realise how upset she's been. And because she's my mum, and because mums are amazing, she tells me not to worry and to enjoy my shopping trip.

"Don't waste all your money on your father and me - we don't need anything," she says.

You get lucky in life or you get unlucky in life. When it came to mums - I've been the luckiest of them all.

CHAPTER NINE

PREPARING FOR CHRISTMAS

"*I* still can't believe you did that," says mum, sitting in her little car with her seat so far forward that her nose is practically touching the windscreen. She wipes a small hole in the condensation that she squints through, like a nocturnal animal peering out into the light for the first time.

"Did what?"

"Oh Mary, you know exactly what I'm talking about - when you rang the tv company a couple of days ago and told them I fed you drugs. I think there's something wrong with you sometimes, I really do."

"I'm sorry," I say, for the thousandth time. "I had a bet with a guy from work that I couldn't get on the show. I shouldn't have done it, you're quite right. I'm sorry mum."

"And what's all the stuff I'm reading about you decorating David Beckham's tree?"

"Yes, it was something I did for work," I say. "They bought a tree from us in the garden centre and I went and decorated it for them."

"Well, everyone's ringing me about it. They say it's been in the papers and everything."

It certainly has. I've done dozens of interviews and the 'Beckham Tree' continues to be Surrey's major tourism attraction, with people coming from far and wide to see it in the gardening centre.

We're quite a ridiculous sight this morning - me and mum - driving to the dump in her little car with the old freezer sticking out the boot (tied on with ropes though God knows whether they'll hold).

"I don't know the way," declares mum. Obviously she has no sat nav, map or even the address of the dump with her. She's so bloody disorganised, but I can't complain really...in that, and in so many other ways...she's exactly like me.

We spent yesterday evening at IKEA - bloody hell, that was a performance and a half. Mum wanted a new freezer and had decided she wanted a massive one - the size of a bloody bungalow. She was dead set on a chest freezer but I managed to talk her out of that; I've seen way too many horror films in which the body ends up in the freezer and gets eaten by the dinner guests. I wanted no part in encouraging cannibalism. But she did insist on one bigger than most restaurants have. There's only the two of them. How much frozen food can one couple eat?

Obviously mum didn't want to pay to have the old one taken away...that's why we're trundling through the backstreets of Cobham with our treacherously large load, hunting for the tip. We've asked three people so far and now appear to be heading in roughly the right direction. Finally, on the side of the road, there's a sign.

"Here mum," I say, confident that she won't have noticed it. "In this entrance on the right."

Mum swings her car down the small side road, recklessly

ignoring all the oncoming traffic as she goes. There are beeped horns and shouts as we disappear from view and mum seems oblivious to all of them.

We pull up on the left hand side in front of a barrier, manned by four guys (four guys! No wonder the economy is in a mess - why does it need four guys to press a button and raise a barrier).

"What you dumping?" asks one of them, like it wasn't entirely plain from the freezer sticking out of the back of the car.

"A freezer," I say.

The man looks down at his clipboard and back up at me.

"And you are hoping to dispose of it?"

"Yes." What else would I be doing? No - it's full of ice cream. I brought it down here to offer you all a nice tasty snack.

"You know you have to phone us in advance if you're bringing white goods, don't you?" he says.

"Who do I have to phone?" I ask.

"Environmental health department," he says. "They are the council's rules, not mine. I don't make the rules, I just do as I'm told."

"Do you have the number?" I ask. There's no way we're taking this freezer back to mum and dad's house. We're leaving it here whether they want it or not. The guy hands me a number and I tap it into my mobile phone. "And what's your name?" I ask him.

"I'm Malcolm," he says. "Head of refuse."

As I wait for someone to answer my call, the phone in the hut starts ringing.

"Excuse me," says Malcolm. "I better just go and get that."

He runs into the shed while I wait for the council to answer my call. Eventually it connects.

"Hello, refuse tip, Malcolm speaking. Can I help you?" he says.

"I want to drop my freezer off at the tip," I say, incredulously. What the hell sort of game is he playing here?

"Sure, where are you?" he asks. "You can bring it down, but there's a backlog of people waiting. Someone's already here with their freezer."

"That's me!" I say. "I'm sitting in the car with my freezer. You told me to call you."

"Great, then you can come through," he says, walking back out again and pressing a button to lift the barrier. "Have a nice day."

IT'S LATE in the evening and I'm looking in the mirror, holding back my cheeks to expose my cheekbones, and lifting my eyebrows to make my eyes look bigger. God, I wish I weren't so fat. You know, the thing with putting on weight is that it affects everything...not just your body. When you think about a fat person you think about the size of their arse and how their stomach sticks out and that they have big thighs...that's all true, but it's also the face. When someone puts on weight it's as if someone has covered their face in uncooked dough...the features become less distinct and the jaw line less clean. There's not a pretty little face with features on it, but a large and rather indistinctive mask. However distinct you look at fighting weight, once you put on the pounds you all start to look the same. You look less like 'you' and more like every other fat person who's ever existed. At least, that's what happened to me.

I found that it wasn't just that I got bigger but my face became a fat person's face and my clothing became that of a fat person - you know - the voluminous dresses and elasticated waists, the retreat into kaftans, always covering the arms, never wearing anything that defines your waist. I'm just a homogenous fat person. I look like every other fat person. All thin people don't look alike, but I fear that all fat people do. No one wants to be like that.

CHAPTER TEN

CHRISTMAS EVE ARRIVES

I leave the store at 3pm on Christmas Eve feeling like a goddess. I wave goodbye to everyone as they cheer my departure in the manner of a famous film star or member of the royal household. They're shouting 'Don't go, don't go.' I feel like Madonna...or I might if I weren't wearing a Father Christmas outfit and being applauded by screaming children while I mutter 'ho, ho, ho.'

Yep, I'm Father Christmas. AGAIN. This task seems to fall to me every year so a variety of reasons but I suspect my size might have something to do with it. I got dragged into the role today because the extra Father Christmas we'd booked arrived looking distinctly dodgy. We'd needed a third Santa because the attention that this place has received over the past few days has been phenomenal and we've got massive waiting lists for the Christmas grotto. Keith wanted to get as many children as possible in to see Santa. The trouble is that the new Santa arrived this morning and it turned out that he had never done this sort of thing before, didn't much like kids and hadn't had any police checks.

"We can't let him go out there and have kids on his

bloody lap if he hasn't been police checked," said Keith. "He could be a complete nonce."

It was hard to argue with the logic. Of course we couldn't have some random bloke out there with kids clambering on his knees one after the other if we didn't know he was safe. The problem was - what would we do about it? Thanks to my efforts in transforming the store into a Christmas paradise, all the children start queuing to get in here at 8am. The car parks are overflowing and you have to queue to see the Beckham Tree in the same way that you have to queue to see the Mona Lisa. My handiwork with pink tinsel is considered a work of art.

Keith and I were standing there and I knew what he was going to say: "Mary, I have a favour to ask you." He leaned over and put his arm around me. "You'd be absolutely great at being Father Christmas. You are a woman so there wouldn't be any hassle with the police checks, and you get on well with kids. Hell, you're even the right shape…"

"Enough about my shape. If you want me to help out, you'd better be kind to me."

"OK, OK, I apologise. Your shape is absolutely perfect. Now, will you please be Father Christmas for me?"

Luckily I had Police checks last year when they wanted me to step in as Santa, so I was ok on that front. I had no desire to play Father Christmas again, but I was keen to make this whole Christmas at the DIY store thing work, and as far as I could see, the only way for that to happen was if I put on the red outfit and made like Santa.

So that's what I've been doing all day, and it's gone well. To be honest – and don't tell Keith this or he'll make me do it every year – I've quite enjoyed it.

He's had to accept that this whole 'put Mary in charge of Christmas' experiment has worked well. Keith is delighted with the publicity we have ended up getting, and takings have been right up (double what we predicted), as people have flocked to the store to see the glorious Beckham Tree. Now I just have to get myself back to the ladies changing room, get dressed and go home, and Christmas can start properly for me. I wave to the children all the way, saying 'ho, ho, ho' in the deepest voice I can muster.

"Don't go, Santa. Don't go," they shout. I've never been so popular in my life as I have these past few days. It's been the most amazing experience. I mean - sure - I've got some things wrong. I wouldn't be Mary Brown if everything had gone perfectly. For example, when it became very busy in the corridors and stairways leading to Santa's grotto, I put up a sign:

*"PLEASE, **when using the stairs:***
  Stay to the right when going up,
  and stay to the left when going down.
  This will keep people from running into each other..."

THAT WASN'T my finest moment, as mothers, fathers and children clutching presents ran head first into those coming down to the grotto clutching their Christmas lists.

So, no, looking back it hasn't all been smooth sailing. But it's over now, and most of it has been great.

I'll be glad to get out of here though. I remove the Father Christmas suit and I put my jeans on, along with boots and a big baggy top, wrapping my scarf around my neck to keep me warm, I feel a wave of excitement about spending the evening with Ted, and waking up with him tomorrow morning. The bit after that is where it gets difficult, because – as you know – I still haven't told him that we are committed to spending Christmas with both sets of parents. I genuinely believe he should tell his mum that we can no longer go there, I can't possibly tell mine after the disaster of me announcing on This Morning that my mum was a drug pusher.

She really will take it personally if I now announce that I'm not coming for Christmas, or that Ted can't make Christmas.

The only alternative I can think of is to go to both sets of parents and have lunch with them all. Ted won't be all that delighted, I don't think. He'd just like to properly go to his parents' house. But I can't think how else we can handle this without causing offence.

Later that night I'm at home with Ted, curled up on the sofa, having wrapped all the presents and feeling wonderful. Ted's watching the news while I laze rather sleepily, sipping my wine.

"You know what I think," he says. "I think that if I were a dictator, I wouldn't have a square."

What?

"A square?"

"Yes - you know - like Red Square and Tiananmen Square...all the problems, uprisings and murders...they always happen in squares. You just shouldn't have one. There you go - that's my tip for dictators."

"Very good," I say, drifting off to sleep. "If I become a dictator, I'll bear that in mind. Oh - and - by the way - I've really cocked up."

"In what way?" asks Ted, innocently.

"I have promised my mum that we will go for Christmas lunch with her tomorrow."

"Whaaaat? Are you serious?" he asks. "You've told your mum we'll be there when you know that I've told my mum that we'll be at hers."

"Yep."

"That's a disaster. I can't cancel mum. She's been shopping and has bought everything already and she did ask first."

"Well, no, technically, I don't think she did. Mine did...and I said 'yes' but then when I arrived at yours, you were so excited about going to your mum's that I couldn't face telling you."

"What are we going to do?" he says. "I don't want us to spend Christmas apart. And I thought your dad didn't like meeting new people."

"He doesn't, and he hates having anyone in the house. All he wants to do is watch programmes about Margaret Thatcher. It's amazing that he's said you can come over. I can't cancel. But - I have a plan."

"Go on."

"Well," I say. "My mum's lunch is at 1pm and yours is at 4pm."

"Two lunches?"

"Unless you can think of a better plan."

"Is there ever a better plan than two lunches?"

CHAPTER ELEVEN

CHRISTMAS MORNING

I wake up most mornings and think 'when can I eat?' I open my eyes and scan the room, and perhaps kiss Ted good morning, but all I can think about is when I'm going to get something to eat. When will I taste hot buttered toast with lashings of peanut butter on top. Thick bread, thick butter, thick peanut butter...big bite. God, I can feel myself salivating at the thought of it.

Food is my overriding concern all the time. If I feel happy I want to celebrate with food and if I feel sad I fall into food, and fill myself with it until I can't feel the pain any more. The thing I want to do more than anything, all the time, is eat. On 364 days of the year I am trying to moderate myself and control myself around food. I wake up every day determined to pace myself and not eat all the day's calories before 8am. I try to leave having meals as late as possible so that I don't have time to eat too much.

But Christmas Day is the one day of the year when I don't have to do any of that, because the day is free of the usual food timing restraints. You can eat what you like, when you want - it's the law. No one can tell you off for having a three sherbet dib-dabs and five jelly babies, or having a bowl of custard before breakfast. It's all allowed. No one will tell you that you are going to spoil your lunch. Nutty food combinations in unspeakable quantities are positively encouraged; you can delight in it... If you say 'I'll have a plain boiled egg,' people will laugh 'no you won't - you'll have Baileys flavoured popcorn and pop tarts dipped in marmite - it's Christmas. What's wrong with you?'

In some ways you'd think this would be a living nightmare for someone like me, with a food addiction, but it's not. It's really not. Once all the rules disappear and I'm not able to beat myself up for breaking them, I find myself feeling much happier and more comfortable with myself. If I have honey ice cream and chips for breakfast that's fine. One a normal day I'll have honey ice cream and chips and hate myself for it, and feel weighed down with guilt and disgust with myself, and it is those feelings of disgust that will push me headlong into food and really cause me problems for days after my one bit of naughty behaviour occurred. It's the disgust that does for me; that's what causes me problems.

Anyway - that little speech was just my long-winded way of telling you that it's 7.30am and I've eaten an entire box of After Eights. I mean - how rebellious is that? It's not even after eight in the morning, let alone after eight in the evening, and all that is left of the previously full box are scattered wrappers and the pungent aroma of fresh mint. I wander into the kitchen and see the bottle of ginger wine on the side. "Oooo..." I think, but - no - even I have some standards. Gurgling ginger wine at the crack of dawn is the route to nowhere good.

"What are you doing up and wandering around, instead of being tucked up in bed next to me?" says Ted, walking into my small kitchen behind me and wrapping his hands around my waist.

"Mmmm...you smell nice," he says. "What is that?"

"After Eights," I reply. See - no shame, no embarrassment, no disgust, no lying to hide my ridiculous eating habits - I just tell Ted quietly and confidently and he doesn't bat an eyelid. "Excellent start to the day," he says. "That ginger wine looks nice."

"I know - I thought that, but that's really a bad idea. We'll both be fast asleep by 10am if we get started on that and we've got two lunches to go to today."

"OK, well why don't I just give you this instead," he says, handing me an envelope. "It's a book token...I didn't know what else to get you."

I try to hide the feeling of disappointment welling up inside me. A book token?

"How nice," I say, gingerly opening the envelope. I don't want any bloody books. I wonder whether I can swap it for cash? Is that really ungrateful?

I pull out the paper inside but it doesn't say anything about books. It's a ticket to Greece for the holiday of a lifetime. I look at Ted open-mouthed...a holiday? Not books?

"Of course it's not books," he says. "I thought it would be nice if we went away on holiday."

"Oh my God, oh my God, oh my God. Best. Present. Ever," I squeal. "This is just amazing."

I feel really bad now that I only got him a jumper and some boxer shorts.

11.30AM:

SANTA HAT? Check.

A huge pile of presents? Check.

A bottle of really strange, green alcohol that I won in a tombola and think mum might like? Check

"Come on then, let's go," I say to Ted, knowing that by now mum will be peering out of the window, desperate for us to arrive.

"Coming," says Ted, walking through the flat with a small bundle of presents.

"What are they for?"

"Well - I might have an extra one or two for you, and I've got presents for your mum and dad - nothing much, just little thank-you gifts for inviting me to join them for lunch."

Bugger.

I have no extra presents for Ted and it never even occurred to me to bring presents for his parents. I'm bloody useless! And I'm Mary Christmas...I'm supposed to be in charge of Christmas.

"Hang on. Hang on," I say.

I have presents under the bed. I've just remembered.

"Be back in a sec," I say to Ted, tearing past him and reaching under the mattress, past the dozens of shoes that I never wear because they are too tight or too high (but they look lovely, so I'm not throwing them away).

There!

Nestling between some candyfloss pink wedges and a pair of way-too-small gold sparkly trainers that no one over the age of four should wear, are three little presents. I can't even remember what's in them...they've been here since last Christmas. It's probably chocolates or a book or some other generic present. Enough to make it look as if I've made an effort without looking like I've gone over the top. I pull them out, drop them into a carrier bag and rush out to join Ted.

"Let's go!" I say.

We squeeze into Ted's car and head off. Neither of us can get the seat belts round us, but we do our customary thing of trying to do it, then shrugging at one another in despair. I'm really looking forward to the day when I can get it round me, it will feel like a tremendous achievement.

Ted heads off with us both just sitting there, wilfully breaking the law as we ease through Cobham streets, heading for mum's house in Esher. Ted's really quiet on the journey and I can tell he's feeling nervous. He hasn't met my mum and dad before; and I imagine that meeting them for the first time on Christmas Day must make it feel all the more daunting.

"Just here on the left," I say, as Ted swings the car into a small space. I look up and can see the curtains flicker a little. I knew it.

Mum's been looking out of the window all morning, waiting for us to arrive. I'm dreading telling her that we have to leave at 3.30pm (we're going to Ted's mum's for Christmas lunch at 4pm, but I'm not telling my mum that so please don't mention it).

"I bet they won't like me," says Ted, sulkily. "They'll probably think you can do much better than me...and they'd be right. You're so lovely, you could have anyone."

"Stop it, Ted. That's not true; I couldn't have anyone else. I'm desperate. That's why I'm with you."

"Oh great, thanks very much."

"I'm joking, Ted. For goodness sake. You know I'm joking, I love you, I think the world of you."

Ted gives me a hug. "Sorry for being sensitive but it really matters to me that I make a good impression on your mum and dad."

"I know. And I love you even more for that," I say. "Just don't expect too much communication from my dad. He's a bit of a nightmare."

"Mine too," says Ted. "Mine too."

Mum answers the door and throws her arms around me,

hugging me closely. "Happy Christmas, darling girl," she says, grinning from ear-to-ear. "A very merry Christmas."

"This is Ted," I say, indicating him, standing nervously by my side clutching the mountain of presents.

"Hello, lovely to meet you," says mum. "Please come in."

Ted follows me into our hallway where the smells of Christmas lunch hang alluringly in the air.

"Smells delicious," he says, and mum smiles warmly. "Thank you."

It's not all quite so cordial when we meet my dad. He just looks Ted up and down and says: "Blimey, Mary. You managed to find a bloke who's fatter than you."

"Indeed," says Ted, apparently unfazed by dad's rudeness. "Nice to meet you, sir."

He then turns to my mum and asks: "Is there anything I can do to help?"

"Honestly, no - it's fine. Everything is under control," says mum.

"I'm quite handy with a carving knife," he says. "So - please say if I can do anything."

"Of course," says mum, demurely. "Thank you, Ted."

And I swear, in that minute, I fell more hopelessly in love with Ted than I've ever fallen in love with anyone before. I think mum did, too. She kind of swooned, and had to hold on to steady herself. Well, it was either a swoon or she'd been at the wine already; hard to tell for sure.

"Ted, please, take a seat," she says, indicating the furniture in front of us. Dad was in his favourite armchair, scowling at us all, there was the small two seater sofa, and the other armchair - old and rundown but madly comfy. Ted, wisely, chose the armchair. He sat down heavily, and smiled at my mum.

"A little Christmas drink?"

"Please," he says.

"Ooooo...look what I've got," I interject, handing her the bottle of bright green liquid that I'd brought with me.

"Great," she says, unconvinced by the lurid colour of the drink. But mum's unfailingly polite and wouldn't want to dismiss the gift, so minutes later she reappears with several glasses of the stuff to hand out. Oh dear, this wasn't the plan. The last thing I wanted was to drink it, I hoped to get rid of it here so mum would have it sitting in her kitchen rather than mine.

"Well," says mum, blinking furiously after taking a swig. "Is this what the young people are drinking these days?"

"I thought it might be nice to try something new," I say, taking a swig and stepping backwards in alarm. It sure has a hell of a bite on it, I feel like my throat has been gnawed by a tiger.

"I'll get a bit more, shall I?" says mum, and I know, in that very moment, that we are all going to get absolutely hammered. The chances of Christmas lunch arriving at anything close to the suggested time, or in anything like an edible state are becoming more and more remote.

But it's Christmas, so we don't worry about those sorts of things. Mum comes back into the room and we get stuck in.

"I'd love some more please," I say. Meanwhile Ted has yet to take a gulp. Everyone is looking at him as he lifts his glass to his mouth and pours some of the acidic solution down his throat.

"No," he squeals, choking and lifting his legs up in some sort of involuntary action to the impact of the liquid. Unfortunately, though, mums old armchair isn't used to quick, unpredictable, violent movements from 25 stone men, and his legs go up just as the backseat goes down behind him. Suddenly he's upside down in a broken arm chair, trapped and struggling to get back onto his feet.

"Oh my goodness," says mum, as she and I rush over to

try and help him up. Ted looks absolutely mortified, as he struggles to get his (huge) arse out of the chair, and get himself upright. The more effort that mum and I are making to assist him, the worse we seem to be making it, so much so that we are forced to admit defeat and step back and watch him struggle and squirm as he scrambles to his feet.

"Well that didn't go well," he says, finally. He's got sticky green liquid all down his shirt and lying on the floor are the remains of mum's favourite armchair. "This isn't the impact I hoped to have," he adds. "I'm really very sorry."

But mum and I are too busy laughing to hear his apologies. The impact of the strong alcohol combined with seeing Ted jammed upside down with legs and arms in the air, has left us crying with mirth. "I don't think I've ever seen anything so funny in my life," I say.

Mum tries to speak but laughter gags her and she just splutters and smiles and when she realises she can't talk at all for laughing, she leaves the room and runs into the kitchen to get more of the terrible drink I bought.

"This is going so terribly badly," mutters Ted. Dad is sitting there watching the scene unfold, mum's laughter can be heard from the kitchen and I'm rather uselessly dabbing at Ted's once white shirt with a tissue I've found on the side.

"I'm really very sorry," says Ted, to dad. "I'm such a bloody clumsy fool."

Ted looks heart-broken. It's clear that he hoped to make a good impression on my parents, and he feels he's completely blown it. "I'm sure you're probably thinking 'who is this big, fat, useless fool'...I'm not usually so unbelievably careless," Ted is saying.

Perhaps it's Ted's contrition that gets to my dad, perhaps it's the taste of the indescribably bad alcohol, or perhaps it's just the festive spirit, but he does what he's never done before - he smiles, then he laughs, then he says to Ted. "Well son, you've certainly broken the ice."

It's bizarre, and unpredictable, but the broken arm chair situation has lifted this family Christmas, with mum and dad smiling and laughing, while Ted continues to apologise profusely for the mess of an armchair by his side.

Next, it's time for the giving of Christmas presents, and we have this bizarre tradition in our house, where my mum gives my dad the same Christmas card every year, and he doesn't remember from year to year. It's always been a joke between me and mum. Dad looks at it, smiles, thanks her for it and puts it on the mantelpiece, oblivious to the fact that he's been given the same card for the past 30 years.

Mum hands the card over to dad and winks at me. Dad opens it (mum invests in a new envelope every year, but that's it). He surveys the dog, reads the message and puts it onto the mantelpiece.

"Ted," he says. "You see that card?"

"Yes," says my boyfriend.

"Well, that dog is about 30 years old, but it hasn't aged a day."

"How do you mean?" asks Ted. I haven't told him about mum's dog card tradition.

"My wife has given me the same bloody card every year since we got married, and she doesn't think I've noticed."

"Ohhhh," mum and I both cry. How the hell has he noticed something like that?

"God, dad. We rely on you to be unobservant at all times. It's heart-breaking that you've started noticing things."

"I notice lots of things," says dad. "I've certainly noticed the bloody card coming every year, but I'm too polite to comment. But now you've brought Ted along and he's started smashing up the furniture, I guess it feels like it might be time to speak up."

"Well I'm very disappointed," I say.

"Me too," says mum. "I'm going to have to go out and buy a new bloody card now."

Mum refills our glasses and we all comment that the sickly sweet, green liquid is really rather palatable after a couple of glasses.

"The more you drink, the better it gets," says mum with a little 'hick'.

"So, tell me about Mary when she was younger," says Ted.

Mum, Ted and I are now sitting in a row on the small sofa, in the absence of any other seating. The whole thing creaked when we all sat down on it, and I'm hoping to God that it doesn't break. That would be too mortifying for words. The truth is that the sofa is built for two small people - not two enormous ones and one normal sized person.

"Well, there was this one time when Mary went abroad. We don't go in much for abroad in this house, so it was quite an occasion," says mum, and I know straight away what bloody story she's going to tell...it's her favourite one.

"Mary was going to fly with 'assisted travel' which means that someone looks after her on the flight. Now, the way they do this is that they clip a tag on the child's coat and give you a code, and you can go online and track your child's journey...see where they are at any time. It's a good system."

"Yes, that sounds like a really good system," agrees Ted.

"But, do you know what our Mary did?"

"No," says Ted, looking over at me.

"As a joke, she took the clip off her blouse, and clipped it onto someone else's bag. That meant that when I went on to the site to check where she was, it brought up a map of the world, and I could see her plane taking off, then veering the wrong way, then flying off to Spain. I was beside myself! I had to ring up the company and I was screaming and saying my little girl was on the wrong flight. It was awful. Awful."

"You little horror," says Ted, shaking his head at me. "How could you do that to your poor mum? Perhaps I can make it up to you with these presents."

Ted pulls out gifts for mum and dad. He hands over the one for mum first and she can't hide her delight.

"How amazing. Thank you so much," she says, turning a deep shade of pink. She tears off the wrapping to reveal a lovely silk scarf. It's very beautiful, with peacock blue and navy swirls through it.

Mum is thrilled. "Thanks so much," she says, wrapping it around her neck. "That's really very kind of you."

Next he hands a package to dad. I'm astonished at his bravery. Really, I struggle to work out what to buy dad. I've no idea how Ted has managed to think of something.

Dad tears off the paper to reveal a book about Margaret Thatcher...he almost drops it in surprise.

"This is great, thanks Ted," he says. "Fascinating woman. Great present. Thanks, son."

"Lunch is ready," says mum, as Ted and I snuggle up a little closer on the sofa. "All come to the table."

We all sit down and survey the mammoth amount of food before us. Mum has no idea that this is the first of our Christmas lunches, so she's pulled out all the stops.

"What will your parents be doing for Christmas lunch?" she asks, as if she's reading my mind.

"They'll just have lunch together," says Ted. "Just mum and dad."

"Were they sad that you wouldn't be with them this year?"

"Yes, a little, but they are glad that I'm spending Christmas with Mary."

"How nice," says mum. "Turkey?"

We are going to have to leave straight after the Queen's speech in order to get to Ted's on time, but as the time rolls round and we're all seated on the tiny sofa waiting for it to start, I have a sudden emotional pang that I don't want to leave mum and dad's. I just don't want to go galloping across to Ted's mum and dad's house when I know how horrible Ted's dad is, and while mine is behaving with such extraordinary friendliness. It feels so cosy sitting next to one another. The absence of an armchair is working out just fine, though it does look like we're waiting for a bus or something. I wish Ted's parents could come here, instead of us going there, but I know his mum's been cooking dinner all morning. We have to make the effort.

The queen's face looms into view on the screen, and we all lean forward a little.

"Do you remember when you thought Prince Philip had a huge bottom," says my Dad, laughing away to himself.

"What's this?" asks Ted.

"Mary heard them say 'three cheers for Prince Philip' and thought they said 'three chairs for Prince Philip'. She thought he must have a massive bottom."

Thanks, Dad.

CHAPTER TWELVE

CHRISTMAS AT TED'S

I walk into Ted's front room, and can see straight away that they have had a change around in the furniture. For a start, they have a new TV, and - Christ alive - it might be the biggest TV I've ever seen. Most of the living room is plasma.

On one hand I feel like congratulating them on having enough money to buy such an enormous television; on the other hand I'm tempted to criticise them for not having enough money to buy a house big enough to go around it…

We exchange hugs and warm greetings of the season, and I sit down on the sofa.

"Here are some nibbles, you must be starving with us having lunch so late," says Ted's mum, handing me a plate with mini sausage rolls, mini chicken satays and other delights on it. "And take this too," she adds, passing me an enormous mixing bowl full of crisps.

"Yum," I say. "Yes – starving."

Ted looks at me like I've gone insane, but I'm not sure what else to do. I don't want to tell her that we've already had one Christmas lunch. I'm sure she'd be offended.

"Shall we play a game before we eat," says Ted's mum, full of enthusiasm. Ted and I think this is a great idea, because we've drunk about four pints of green alcohol, but Ted's dad is less convinced. He just grunts.

"It'll be fun," she insists.

"No it won't," he says.

I glance at Ted and he raises his eyebrows. Ted's dad makes my parents look positively sociable. I feel really sorry for Ted's mum, she's trying so hard. Ted's dad just sits there and doesn't engage us at all. It's all down to her to make the day work.

"I'm not playing any bloody games. Let's just eat."

"Sure," Ted's mum says, leaving the room and rushing into the kitchen. My God, I feel sorry for her. I run after her and offer to help.

"No dear, honestly, you go back in there and have a good time…" But she looks sad and broken down by the pressure of dealing with Ted's dad.

I go back into the sitting room where Ted and his father are sitting in uncomfortable silence.

I have some presents for you," I say, digging into my bag and pulling out the wrapped Christmas presents that I had retrieved from under the bed earlier.

"Here you go," I say, handing over a gift to Ted's father.

Ted's mum has come into the room behind me, so I turn and hand her I carefully wrapped package as well.

"Thank you dear," she says, turning to her husband: "Isn't that kind of Mary?"

"But what is it?" says Ted's dad. He has opened his package to find a pretend aeroplane inside it. It's brightly painted and made of plastic. He throws it across the room and we all watch as it glides and dips and flies.

"That's a lovely present," says Ted's mum, though I detect the confusion in her voice.

I feel myself go scarlet. Why the hell have I got kid's presents under my bed? I don't know any kids... Oh! I remember now, the presents were from when I played Father Christmas last year. They are the gifts I was giving out in the grotto, and there were too many of them, so I brought a few home. There is no chance on earth that the present that Ted's mum is about to open will be any more appropriate for her than the aeroplane was for Ted's dad. Shit.

"Goodness, that's nice. It might be a bit small though," she says, having opened the package to reveal a cowboy outfit.

Ted is just staring at me. "Do you want to talk us through this?" he says, as his mum makes a valiant attempt to wear a cowboy hat and pin the sheriff's badge onto her dress.

"I'm so sorry," I say. "I saw that Ted had gifts for my mum and dad and I really wanted to bring something for you. I knew there were presents under my bed, so went to get them. I've just remembered that they were presents for children. I'm such an idiot. I thought they were boxes of chocolates. I'm really sorry."

"No, not at all," says Ted's mum. "You know what they say, it's the thought that counts."

"Don't worry," says Ted, hugging me. "Mum's going to look cracking in her new outfit."

Ted's dad is just sitting in an almighty, slovenly heap. I'm starting to miss the relative warmth and happiness of my house.

"You know what we should do after lunch," I say. "We should invite my parents over to join us...then we could play games and have a really lovely time."

"Oh dear, that would be marvellous," says Ted's mum, positively beaming with excitement.

"Let me go and call them," I say.

"Are you sure?" asks Ted. "I mean - will they want to come?"

"I'll find out," I say, and I head out of the room to make the silliest call in the world ever..I have to confess to mum and dad that we are at Ted's for our second Christmas lunch of the day, and I have to ask them to come over in an hour and join us, but they mustn't mention the first lunch.

"Please mum," I say. "I know it's a lot to ask, but it would really make Christmas wonderful. I promise I'll explain all afterwards. Is that OK?"

"Of course it is, dear," says mum. "I'll tell your dad."

She takes the address and says they will be here in an hour.

I walk into the kitchen where Ted's mum is shaking a pan that is laden with roast potatoes. "They are coming," I tell her, and the look on her face says everything...she's delighted not to have to spend the day coping with her husband's miserable attitude, and to have lots of other people to entertain.

"Let me tell everyone."

She runs into the front room and announces that my parents are coming over.

"Oh great," says Ted's dad, unenthusiastically.

"Oh," says Ted. "I see. Mary, can I have a word?"

Ted and I disappear into the back room and I tell Ted how sad his mum looked and how much I'd like to cheer her up.

"If my parents come we can play games and it'll be noisy and fun and Christmassy. Your mum will love it."

"You are lovely," says Ted, hugging me. "But won't they tell Mum that we were there earlier?"

"Mum's promised not to say anything," I explain. "Let's just make Christmas come alive for your mum."

"Thank you," says Ted. "Now, can I ask you something?"

"Yes," I say.

"Will you move in with me? Can we live together...you

know - sometime soon. I mean - not immediately - but...in the future?"

"Oh my God, Ted, I'd love to. I'd really, really love to."

"That's sorted then," he says. "You and me - setting up home together. Happy Christmas Mary Brown."

"Happy Christmas, darling Ted," I say.

Best. Christmas. Ever.

I HOPE YOU ENJOYED THE BOOK!

*T*here are loads more books in the Adorable Fat Girl series & lots more being released all the time. Here are the books in the series that are OUT NOW:

BOOK ONE: Diary of an Adorable Fat Girl

Mary Brown is funny, gorgeous and bonkers. She's also about six stone overweight. When she realises she can't cross her legs, has trouble bending over to tie her shoelaces without wheezing like an elderly chain-smoker, and discovers that even her hands and feet look fat, it's time to take action. But what action? She's tried every diet under the sun.

This is the story of what happens when Mary joins 'Fat Club' where she meets a cast of funny characters and one particular man who catches her eye.

BOOK TWO: Adventures of an Adorable Fat Girl

Mary can't get into any of the dresses in Zara (she tries and fails. It's messy!). Still, what does she care? She's got a lovely new boyfriend whose thighs are bigger than her's (yes!!!) and all is looking well...except when she accidentally gets herself into several thousand pounds worth of trouble at the silent auction, has to eat her lunch under the table in the pub because Ted's workmates have spotted them, and suffers the indignity of having a young man's testicles dangled into her face on a party boat to Amsterdam. Oh, and then there are all the issues with the hash-cakes and the sex museum. Besides all those things - everything's fine...just fine!

BOOK THREE: Crazy Life of an Adorable Fat Girl

The second course of 'Fat Club' starts and Mary reunites with the cast of funny characters who graced book one. But this time there's a new Fat Club member...a glamorous blonde who Mary takes against.

We also see Mary facing troubles in her relationship with the wonderful Ted, and we discover why she has been suffering from an eating disorder for most of her life. What traumatic incident in Mary's past has caused her all these problems?

The story is tender and warm, but also laugh-out-loud funny. It will resonate with anyone who has dieted, tried to keep up with any sort of exercise programme or spent 10 minutes in a changing room trying to extricate herself from a way too-small garment that she ambitiously tried on and is now completely stuck in.

BOOK FOUR: FIRST THREE BOOKS COMBINED

This is the first three Fat Girl books altogether in one fantastic, funny package

BOOK FIVE: Christmas with Adorable Fat Girl

It's the Adorable Fat Girl's favourite time of year and she embraces it with the sort of thrill and excitement normally reserved for toddlers seeing jelly tots. Our funny, gorgeous and bonkers heroine finds herself dancing from party to party, covered in tinsel, decorating the Beckhams' Christmas tree, dressing up as Father Christmas, declaring live on This

Morning that she's a drug addict and enjoying two Christmas lunches in quick succession. She's the party queen as she stumbles wildly from disaster to disaster. A funny little treasure to see you smiling through the festive period.

BOOK SIX: Adorable Fat Girl shares her Weight Loss Tips

as well as having a crazy amount of fun at Fat Club, Mary also loses weight...a massive 40lbs!! How does she do it? Here in this mini book - for the first time - she describes the rules that helped her. Also included are the stories of readers who have written in to share their weight loss stories. This is a kind approach to weight loss. It's about learning to love yourself as you shift the pounds. It worked for Mary Brown and everyone at Fat Club (even Ted who can't go a day without a bag of chips and thinks a pint isn't a pint without a bag of pork scratchings). I hope it works for you, and I hope you enjoy it.

BOOK SEVEN: Adorable Fat Girl on Safari

Mary Brown, our fabulous, full-figured heroine, is off on safari with an old school friend. What could possibly go wrong? Lots of things, it turns out. Mary starts off on the wrong foot by turning up dressed in a ribbon bedecked bonnet, having channeled Meryl Streep from Out of Africa. She falls in lust with a khaki-clad ranger half her age and ends up stuck in a tree wearing nothing but her knickers, while sandwiched between two inquisitive baboons. It's never dull...

BOOK EIGHT: Cruise with an Adorable Fat Girl

Mary is off on a cruise. It's the trip of a lifetime...featuring eat-all-you-can buffets and a trek through Europe with a 96-year-old widower called Frank and a flamboyant Spanish dancer called Juan Pedro. Then there's the desperately hand-some captain, the appearance of an ex-boyfriend on the ship, the time she's mistaken for a Hollywood film star in Lisbon and tonnes of clothes shopping all over Europe.

BOOK NINE: Adorable Fat Girl Takes up Yoga

The Adorable Fat Girl needs to do something to get fit. What about yoga? I mean - really - how hard can that be? A bit of chanting, some toe touching and a new leotard. Easy! She signs up for a weekend retreat, packs up assorted snacks and heads for the countryside to get in touch with her chi and her third eye. And that's when it all goes wrong. Featuring frantic chickens, an unexpected mud bath, men in loose-fitting shorts and no pants, calamitous headstands, a new bizarre friendship with a yoga guru and a quick hospital trip.

BOOK TEN FIRST THREE HOLIDAY BOOKS COMBINED

This is a combination book containing three of the books in my holiday series: Adorable Fat Girl on Safari, Cruise with an Adorable Fat Girl and Adorable Fat Girl takes up Yoga.

BOOK ELEVEN: Adorable Fat Girl and the Mysterious Invitation

Mary Brown receives an invitation to a funeral. The only problem is: she has absolutely no idea who the guy who's died is. She's told that the deceased invited her on his deathbed, and he's very keen for her to attend, so she heads off to a dilapidated old farm house in a remote part of Wales. When she gets there, she discovers that only five other people have been invited to the funeral. None of them knows who he is either.

NO ONE GOING TO THIS FUNERAL HAS EVER HEARD OF THE DECEASED.

Then they are told that they have 20 hours to work out why they have been invited in order to inherit a million pounds.

Who is this guy and why are they there? And what of the ghostly goings on in the ancient old building?

BOOK TWELVE Adorable Fat Girl goes to weight loss camp

Mary Brown heads to Portugal for a weight loss camp and discovers it's nothing like she expected. "I thought it would be Slimming World in the sunshine, but this is bloody torture," she says, after boxing, running, sand training (sand training?), more running, more star jumps and eating nothing but carrots. Mary wants to hide from the instructors and cheat the system. The trouble is, her mum is with her, and won't leave her alone for a second. Then there's the angry instructor with the deep, dark secret about why he left the army; and the mysterious woman who sneaks into their pool and does synchronised swimming every night. Who the hell is she? Why's she in their pool? And what about Yvonne - the slim, attractive lady who disappears every night after dinner. Where's she going? And what unearthly difficulties will Mary get herself into when she decides to follow her to find out…

BOOK THIRTEEN: The first two weight loss books:
This is Weight loss tips and Weight loss camp together

OR, is romance your thing?

IF IT IS, see my new romantic novels under the pen name, Rosie Taylor-Kennedy - I've written a series of books about four sisters who live together in Sunshine Cottage in a beautiful village called 'Cove Bay.' It's like Little Women for the modern reader!

. . .

AND THERE ARE lots more books on the way, including Mary's Road Trip to USA with Ted and another mystery for Mary to solve, called Adorable Fat Girl and the Mysterious Pregnancy, and Confessions of an Adorable Fat Girl

… Then there's the relaunch of a very funny series of books about Wags…

See the website here: www.bernicebloom.com

(if you click onto it, you can get a free book!)

A FINAL WORD

Do make sure you come and join us on Facebook. There's a Bernice Bloom group that is full of great, fun women:

https://www.facebook.com/BerniceBloombooks

Thank you so much for all your support

Bernie xx

Published by Gold Medals Media Ltd

Bernice Bloom has asserted her right to be identified as the author of this
Work in accordance with the Copyright, Designs and Patents Act 1988

This novel is a work of fiction.

❀ Created with Vellum

Printed in Great Britain
by Amazon